Sailing for Adventure

Adapted (loosely) by Alison Inches
From the movie *Muppet Treasure Island*
Original screenplay by Jerry Juhl & Kirk R. Thatcher and James V. Hart
Based (very, very loosely) on the novel by Robert Louis Stevenson

MUPPET PRESS

Grosset & Dunlap · New York

Copyright © 1996 Jim Henson Productions, Inc.
All rights reserved. No part of this book may be reproduced or copied in any form without written
permission from the copyright owner. MUPPET TREASURE ISLAND logo, MUPPET, MUPPET
PRESS, and character names and likenesses are trademarks of Jim Henson Productions, Inc.
Published by Grosset & Dunlap, Inc., a member of The Putnam & Grosset Group, New York.
GROSSET & DUNLAP is a trademark of Grosset & Dunlap, Inc. Published simultaneously in Canada.
Printed in the U.S.A. Library of Congress Number: 95-79177
ISBN 0-448-41275-6   A B C D E F G H I J

It was nearly closing time at The Admiral Benbow Inn. A salty old sea captain looked up from his grog. Billy Bones he was called. He was telling a story about a treasure buried on a faraway island and a pirate named Flint.

"A-r-r-rgh!" Billy growled. "Ol' Flinty up and died 'afore he could dig up his treasure. And to this day, no one knows who has his map."

Jim Hawkins, a poor orphan boy, and his friends Rizzo and Gonzo had been listening to Billy's tale. "If I had that map," said Jim, "I sure wouldn't be working here, Mr. Bones."

"That's right," added Gonzo. "We'd be out sailing the seven seas searching for that treasure!"

Later that night, Jim and his friends heard a loud
CRASH! An ugly pirate was breaking down the door. He'd
come looking for Captain Bones.

"I know you have the map," the pirate shouted.

And it was true. Billy Bones did have the map. He'd had it all along!

"Take it—*and run!*" Billy cried, giving the map to Jim. "But remember: Beware the one-legged man! He be the one to fear."

Jim grabbed the map and raced out of the inn with Gonzo and Rizzo—just in time to escape the pirate!

When Jim and his friends finally stopped running, they agreed there was only one thing to do: *Find the treasure!* So off they hurried to see young Squire Trelawney. He was very rich and loved adventure.

"Treasure, you say? And pirates?" said the squire. "Well, that settles it. We'll take my boat, the *Hispaniola! Olé!*"

On board the *Hispaniola*, Jim and his friends stared in surprise.

"The captain is a frog!" said Jim.

"That's nothing," said Gonzo. "Check out the crew!"

The three friends watched as the creepy-looking crew hoisted the sails. Then the frog captain took the helm. And with a *Yo, ho, ho!* they were off!

Down in the galley, Jim met the ship's cook, Long John Silver. Jim liked him right away. Then Long John came out from behind his counter. *Clump–clump–clump!* He was missing one leg!

Could Long John Silver be the one-legged man Billy Bones had warned them about? *Naw*, Jim thought. Mr. Silver seemed much too nice.

But Jim was wrong! Long John Silver *was* a rotten pirate—and so was the crew. They were after the treasure map. And Jim didn't even know it.

But Captain Smollett had grown suspicious. "We'd better keep that treasure map of yours a secret," he told Jim. So, just to be safe, he locked Jim's map up in his cabin.

But that didn't stop Long John! As soon as he found out where the map was hidden, Long John snuck into Captain Smollett's cabin to steal it.

The next day, Jim, Rizzo, and Gonzo overheard the pirates talking. "Now that we have Jim's map, me hearties, the riches will soon be mine—*I mean ours.*" It was Long John Silver!

Rizzo and Gonzo and Jim could not believe their ears. Long John Silver *was* the one-legged man Billy Bones had warned them about!

Just then, a voice from on deck cried, "*Land ho-o-o-o-o!*"

Jim, Rizzo, and Gonzo ran to find Captain Smollett.

"Captain!" Jim cried. "Long John Silver has stolen the map. Now he's planning to take over the ship!"

Captain Smollett thought for a moment. Then he calmly ordered the crew to go ashore for food and water. "As soon as the pirates get to shore," he told Jim, "we'll set sail for home and return later with an honest crew."

It was a good plan, but there was one problem. Long John Silver kidnapped Jim and took him ashore, too!

"We've got to rescue Jim!" said his friends. So Captain Smollett, Rizzo, and Gonzo jumped into a jolly boat and headed for shore.

When they landed, they were greeted by a tribe of wild boars. "Howdy do, stinky frog man and friends," said the boar king. "You trespass on island. Now you suffer wrath of our queen, Boom Sha-Kal-a-Kal!"

The queen rode in on a huge elephant. "Thank you, thank you," she said, blowing kisses all around. Then she saw Captain Smollett. "Smolly?" she cried. "Can it be you?" This was no goddess. This was the captain's old girlfriend, Benjamina Gunn!

Meanwhile, on the other side of the island, Long John and the pirates had found Flint's treasure chamber. But when they opened the chests—*avast!*—they were empty!

Now the pirates were mad! And the best thing to do when you're around mad pirates is run for your life. So that's just what Jim did.

But that wasn't the last of the pirates. *Oh, no!* Long John Silver had a hunch that Benjamina could tell him where the treasure was.

"Where is the treasure, Benjamina!" Long John demanded. "Tell me, or I'll flog the frog!" He grabbed Captain Smollett by the throat.

"Don't hurt my frog, you scoundrel!" she squealed. "The treasure is at my place!"

"A-ha!" laughed Long John. Then he tied up the captain and Benjamina and hung them over a cliff by their feet!

   The pirates made a dash for Benjamina's bungalow,
where they found Flint's treasure—every golden bit!
   Meanwhile, Jim found Rizzo and Gonzo and helped
them escape from the wild boars. As the three friends
made their way back to the ship, they plotted a way to get
back the treasure.

On board the *Hispaniola* once again, Jim took the helm.
First he sailed toward Benjamina and Captain Smollett.
And just in time! *Snap!* Their ropes broke, and down they
fell into the waiting ship. Then Jim headed straight for the
pirates.

Scr-r-r-runch! The ship ran aground and out leapt Jim and his friends, armed with cutlasses, cannonballs—and a few starfish!

"On guard, rapscallions!" cried Jim.

"Take that, you swab!" shouted Rizzo.

And before you could say, *"Blow me down!"* the pirates were defeated.

The brave and victorious Captain Smollett locked Long
John and the other pirates away in the ship's jail. Then
they loaded up the treasure and set sail for home.

But—*shiver me timbers*—the prison bars were loose! Slippery Long John Silver escaped—with two big treasure chests . . . and one very leaky lifeboat!

"So long, Long John!" called Jim. "Hello, fortune and adventure!"